Hello Huckleberry Heights

OTHER YEARLING BOOKS
YOU WILL ENJOY:

YEARLING BOOKS/YOUNG YEARLINGS/YEARLING CLASSICS are designed especially to entertain and enlighten young people. Patricia Reilly Giff, consultant to this series, received the bachelor's degree from Marymount College. She holds the master's degree in history from St. John's University, and a Professional Diploma in Reading from Hofstra University. She was a teacher and reading consultant for many years, and is the author of numerous books for young readers.

For a complete listing of all Yearling titles, write to Dell Readers Service, P.O. Box 1045, South Holland, IL 60473.

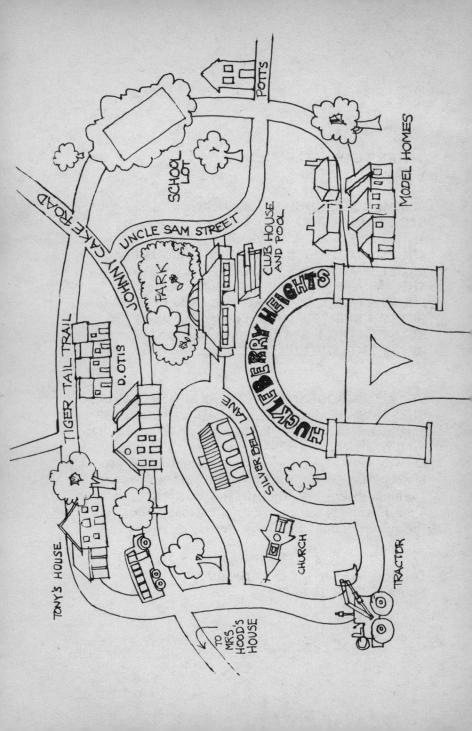

Hello Huckleberry Heights

Judy Delton

Illustrated by Alan Tiegreen

A YEARLING BOOK

Published by
Dell Publishing
a division of
Bantam Doubleday Dell Publishing Group, Inc.
666 Fifth Avenue
New York, New York 10103

Text copyright © 1990 by Judy Delton
Illustrations copyright © 1990 by Alan Tiegreen
Design by SNAP-HAUS GRAPHICS, Diane Stevenson

ISBN: 0-440-40304-9

Printed in the United States of America

July 1990

10 9 8 7 6 5 4 3 2 1

CWO

*FOR KATHERINE GREENE LEWIS, WITH THANKS
FOR THE JOY HER POETRY HAS BROUGHT ME*

And with thanks to editor Lori Mack

And acknowledgment to Elliot Katz, Esq.

HUCKLEBERRY HEIGHTS, said the big block letters in the arch. Underneath, another sign said LOW DOWN PAYMENT TO QUALIFIED BUYERS. CONDOMINIUMS FOR MODERN LIVING.

The arch looked like the entrance to an amusement park, or Disney World or something. There were big wooden columns on each side. The letters of HUCKLEBERRY HEIGHTS were all different colors.

But we weren't in Florida. We were in St. Paul, Minnesota. I've lived here my whole life, ten years. My name is Tony Doyle.

My mom drove our car under the arch and pulled up in front of a big house that looked occupied. It had curtains in the windows and lights on, even though it was the middle of the afternoon. I knew no one really lived there, because it said MODEL HOME on a sign in the front yard. These houses looked big on the outside. But inside they were smaller. That was because each one was really divided into four houses, called condominiums. Condo for short. Each condo had its own front and back door that opened onto the yard. And most of them had their own upstairs and basement.

I saw a lot of model homes. My mom said it was getting too expensive to rent. She wanted to buy a condo. So we drove around every Sunday (bor-ing) looking at these houses instead of going to a movie or eating a big Sunday dinner like other kids did. (My mom's idea of a

2

big Sunday dinner is take-out ginger chicken wings from Lee Ann Chin's.)

"It's too windy out here," said my sister, Marcy, who is twelve. She pulled her jacket up over her ears.

"The trees are too short," said my little brother, Gus. "No good for climbing." Gus is eight.

"It's dirty," I said as the car sank into the mud in front of the model home. "It's not a model street."

"It's wonderful!" said my mother. "I think we'll buy it!"

My sister groaned. My brother started to cry. I said, "Mom, we haven't even seen the inside yet!"

If it weren't for me, our family would be a disaster. My mother's slightly impulsive. She just doesn't think about things ahead of time. Like a grocery list. If I didn't make one, she'd buy all this snack stuff that would be gone in one day and our teeth would be rotted. A mother's supposed to think of things like that. But my mom doesn't. She never has. It's always been up to me. My little brother is no help, he's a baby. And my big sister is one of those people who write poems and draw pictures and try on clothes for hours in Dayton's, but what good is she in a crisis?

As I say, it's up to me. I have to be the man of the house. (My parents are divorced and my dad lives in California.)

"What about taxes?" I demanded. "And how many bedrooms are there?"

"You said if we had a house we could all have our own room," said Gus from the backseat.

"Oh, I'm sure there are all kinds of bedrooms, Fergus," said my mother vaguely. My mother did not believe in nicknames.

"What about schools, and where is the grocery store?" I said. Where we lived, I ran to Crossfield's ten times a day for something my mom forgot. It was a store just below us in our big apartment building.

My mom leaned on the steering wheel. She squinted her eyes and tapped her teeth with her fingernail the way she does when she is thinking. I hate it when she thinks. It means she is going to do something we'll be sorry about.

"This is our house," she said. "Just think, kids. We will have a yard with green grass. A barbecue in the back. We can plant flowers. Maybe we can even get a dog!"

"And who would take care of it?" I said. "I've got homework and stuff to do."

"And who would plant the flowers?" said my sister. She comes down to earth when my mother makes plans, because she knows they could involve her.

"The association tends lawns and shovels snow," said my mother.

"I want a dog!" shouted Gus.

My mom turned the car into the driveway and parked. The minute we stepped

out of the car, we sank into mud over our shoes.

"Yuck!" said my sister. "I definitely don't want to live out here!"

I looked down the street. Every yard was mud. There was a big tractor standing like a yellow dinosaur. A dead dinosaur. Some condos were finished. Some only had two-by-fours and you could see inside them. It made me lonely for our nice apartment in the city.

"Let's go home," wailed Gus. "I don't want a dog if we have to live in the mud."

But my mom was already in the front door shaking the real estate man's hand. We followed her in, walking on the plastic runner they put down in model houses.

"Welcome to Huckleberry Heights," the real estate man was saying. "The home of modern Americans."

"What kind of heat does the house have?" I asked. (It's up to me to check things out.) "Is the garage included in the price?" I had heard people ask these questions in other model homes. My mom was already down the hall asking about the appliances.

"Are the washer and dryer included?" I asked. I jotted his answers down in my notebook. My sister stood and filed her fingernails. Gus was on his way down the basement stairs. "A dog could live down here!" he called.

"We'll take it," said my mother, as if she were buying a pound of roast beef at the market.

"Mom," I whispered in her ear. "This is a house, not a box of cereal. You better think about it. We should go home and vote or something."

But my mom was already signing some paper. Probably one of those things they warn you about on TV. With the small print.

The real estate man was smiling. No

one else was buying his condos this fast. "You realize, Mrs. Doyle—"

"Ms.," my mother interrupted.

"You realize, Ms. Doyle, that it isn't this very house you will be buying."

"This is just the model," I said. "Number 459. Two-story family dwelling."

"I know that," said my mother quickly so we wouldn't think she was dumb.

The man showed her a little plastic model of the whole neighborhood. It was set up on the dining room table. "Right here," he said, pointing between two make-believe pine trees and a building that looked like a church. "You'll get a nice breeze up on this hill in the summer."

Gus was running his Matchbox car down the little streets on the plastic model. "Vrooommm."

Mom wrote a check for something called earnest money and then herded us all out the door to where the car was a little deeper in the mud. The three of us and the real estate man had to push it while she spun the back wheels.

"Well!" Mom said as we sped down the freeway back to town. "Wasn't that fun? Won't it be great to live in the country? Aren't we the luckiest family alive to be moving into a house like that? Room to run. And new friends to meet. Healthy, unpolluted air."

"I hate it," said my sister. "I don't want to move! I just got on our pep squad, and our 6th-grade festival is coming up!"

"There will be pep squads and festivals in Huckleberry Heights," said my mother.

We groaned. Marcy wouldn't know anyone. I wouldn't know anyone. We would be a million miles from a store or a library. I knew it would be me who would have to take care of the dog. The dog my mom would have to promise Gus to get him to move.

Our apartment started to feel real nice to me now. The familiar noises in the night, Mr. Holmes coming home late from his poker parties, Tommy Sill practicing his violin. I sighed. The things we did for our mother.

You are probably wondering how my mom can afford to buy this house. I didn't tell you about her job.

My mom runs a faucet company. It is just a small specialty company, but it is hers. "Just look at this!" she would say, putting her arm around me when I was trying to do my math. "Did you ever see a shine like that? It comes in gold, bronze, silver, and pewter."

"It's wonderful," I always say, fingering her faucet. "I can see my face in it."

People like my mom's faucets. They have them installed in new houses. And sometimes they tear out all the faucets in their old homes and have hers put in. There are lots of her faucets in Huckleberry Heights already. My mom's whole life is faucets.

She is good at her work, but she's so forgetful. I have this dream that someday my mom is going to make some giant mistake and I'll have to bail her out of jail. "Oh, does the decimal point go *there*," she'll say. "I thought the bankbook said a thousand dollars! Is it really only a hundred?"

I often think I should quit school and get a job to be on the safe side. But what can a kid my age do to earn enough to take care of four people and a house and maybe even a dog?

That night I took my calendar down from the wall and put a big circle around next month. Then I wrote, "This is when my life ends. We are moving to a place called Huckleberry Heights. (What in the world are huckleberries?) I wish I was dead."

The days went by and my mom's check didn't bounce and the real estate man said we could move in the first of the month. We started to pack. Marcy cried as she put her perfume bottles in a box.

"All that fresh air!" my mom kept saying over and over, as if that was all that mattered.

After two weeks we were beginning to look forward to moving. Marcy wasn't crying anymore. Crying was one of those things you couldn't keep up forever even if you tried.

My mom's friends and relatives came to help us pack. And some of the people from her faucet company. (The company was called Trixie's Taps—that's my mom's name, Trixie. She always wanted us to call her that, but we never did. I prefer "Mom.")

"Good-bye walls," Gus said the last night. "Good-bye lights. Good-bye steps. Good-bye sink. Good-bye bathtub."

"Good-bye Gus!" we said in a high, squeaky bathtub voice. "I'll miss you," we said in the voice of the toilet.

In the morning we said good-byc to the neighbors and the kids we played with. We ate take-out muffins and watched for the van.

"It's here!" screamed Gus. A giant moving van turned onto our street.

All of a sudden my mom began to cry. "What have we done?" she wailed. "Why are we moving out of our nice cozy apartment? Away from all of our friends? I'll have such a long drive to work. Why didn't you stop me?" she sobbed.

Marcy and I stared at her. I wanted to shake her. I wanted to say, Why did you sign those papers? Why did you pay money down so fast?

But I didn't. I just put my arm around her and said, "Think of all that fresh air, Mom. And the yard and the barbecue."

"Trust us," said Marcy. "You'll love it."

2

"Can I ride with the furniture?" shouted Gus when the van was loaded. One of the men pulled him up onto the cab when no one said no.

We followed the van, and behind us came cars with my mom's friends and my aunt Fluffy. They were going to help us move in. We drove on the freeway and under the arch. We passed the model houses and turned down the curvy street where our house, model 459, was. It was called Tiger Tail Trail.

We passed the yellow dinosaur. "Our street should be called Dinosaur Street," said Marcy. The big yellow bulldozer never moved.

We passed houses that men were pounding on. We passed empty lots. We passed a couple of finished houses that had mailboxes in front of them and curtains in the windows.

And then the moving van made wheezing noises and slowed down in front of model 459.

"Who's that kid?" I said.

A boy wearing blue jeans tumbled down our rutted driveway.

In a flash he was up on the side of the van talking to the driver. Then he jumped down and began to direct the truck into the rutted driveway. The driver backed in carefully, avoiding the deepest ruts that the boy pointed out. He made motions with his fingers to come toward him.

"Slow, slow, slow . . ." he called. Then

he held up his hands, palms out, saying, *"Stop!"* The van lurched to one side and came to a stop before it hit our new garage, included in the price of model 459.

My mother stuck her head out the window.

"I'm Lenny Fox," the kid said before my mom could ask. "I live in a 459 just like yours a block away on Johnny Cake Road. I'm eight."

"What a nice boy you are, Leonard!" said my mother.

Then she turned to us and said. "Just look at that. A friend for Anthony, and Fergus, right off the stick!"

"Bat," I said. "Off the bat."

My mom always gets those sayings wrong, but we watch *Wheel of Fortune* and try to set her straight.

We parked the car in the smallest rut, and got out to see our house. The wind almost blew us over. My mom's hair stood straight up on her head, as if she had seen a ghost. She took out a key, and we climbed the steps with all the helpers behind us and walked into the whitest, cleanest living room I'd ever seen. It looked bigger than the model homes. That was probably because it was totally bare. It smelled damp.

"Wonderful!" said a faucet man.

"Spacious!" said our aunt.

They directed all the furniture traffic and swept the kitchen floor and carried plastic buckets around.

But Marcy and I just stood there like refugees in a new land where we didn't speak the language. We could hear Gus outside with Lenny Fox. And the wind blowing. But inside it was quiet as a tomb. I shivered.

"I love it," said Marcy softly.

"It's okay," I admitted.

"There *is* more room." my mother admitted. I knew she'd come around.

"What a wonderful broom closet!" said a muffled voice from the kitchen. It sounded hollow like a ghost, but it was just my aunt Fluffy. She's my mom's sister. She got her name Fluffy because her blond hair fluffs out a lot. Otherwise she looks just like Mom.

As we stood there the men brought in the couch. And the chairs. And our beds and mattresses. It was embarrassing to see all our personal stuff sitting right outside in the daylight for everyone to look at. A big crowd was gathering outside. One nice lady pushed through the crowd with a chocolate cake for us. Another one brought a tuna casserole.

I noticed that my mom had already forgotten she didn't want to live here.

"Just smell that good food!" she said to us.

When I opened the screen door to go out to get a box, the wind grabbed it out of my hand. It snapped off its hinges and sailed away with a crash.

"Mom!" Marcy shouted. "Tony's wrecking our new house already!"

But my mom was busy investigating her new bedroom and just called, "We will get a little man to fix it." She always called repairmen "little men," even though sometimes the men who came to fix things were six feet tall.

When I finally went to get the box, Gus and Lenny were sitting in the cab of the van playing driver. They made roaring noises and turned the wheel. "Zooooom!" called Gus.

"Hey, you kids . . ." I shouted. "You could release something by mis—"

That was as far as I got. The truck lurched to one side and began to roll. Not down the drive. Or into the garage door. But right into our "lawn" of mud. Then it stopped.

The moving men dashed out of the house and grabbed the kids from the cab and dumped them out fast into mud. They sank in to their knees. Their legs and feet were black, but their faces were white as sheets.

"We'll never get this thing out of your lawn," said the driver, shaking his head at the truck.

"We'll never have a lawn," I said, looking at the wheels that had bulldozed a hole big enough for another basement.

"I didn't do it!" yelled Gus.

"We both did it," said Lenny.

The driver pulled the kids out of the mud, but their shoes stayed there.

The movers looked nervous. They were eager to unload everything and leave.

After another hour had passed and all the things were in the house, they left.

"No water comes out of the bathroom faucet upstairs," said Marcy, coming down the steps.

"I'm sure water comes with the house," said my mother.

"There's water in *my* room," said Gus.

"Oh, great," I said.

We all ran to Gus's room. He was right. Water was drip drip dripping onto his bed from the ceiling. My aunt Fluffy put a pan under it.

"Condensation," she said wisely. "Hot and cold condenses. The air is cold and the sun is hot."

It's easy to tell that Fluffy is my mom's sister.

"We'll get a little man to fix it," said my mother.

"Nothing ever broke in the apartment," said Marcy.

I poked Marcy. It was our job to keep our mother's spirits up. And she knew it.

All the helpers unpacked the stuff we needed the most. Like plates and silverware. I put sheets on the beds and mopped up water and plaster dust. My bed looked lonely in the middle of my white bedroom. When we called to one another, our voices echoed, the house seemed so empty. I wondered if I'd be able to sleep with all this space around me. Empty white air. In the apartment all I'd had to do was reach out my arm to touch Gus's bed, or my highboy. Here I'd have to get out of my bed and walk a mile to touch anything at all.

"Supper!" called Aunt Fluffy.

We all sat around the table and ate the casserole and cake and some carrot sticks, and then the helpers hugged my mom and said, "Call if you need us." Then they were gone.

No one had moved into the other condos in our building. We were all alone in Huckleberry Heights.

Just as it was growing dark, the front doorbell rang. A woman was standing there holding a basket with a napkin over it.

"More food!" said Marcy. "I hope it's a pie!"

"I'm Mrs. Fox," said the woman.

"Lenny's mother. Gus has been telling us that his mother said he could have a dog, and our dog has had puppies. We thought this might be a nice housewarming gift for you."

She handed Mom the basket. The napkin began to move. A furry little nose pushed it out of the way. I could see that it was a sheepdog puppy!

"My *dog*!" shouted Gus, shooting across the room. He lifted him out of the basket and hugged him. "Thank you!" he said to Lenny's mother.

"You'll have to put papers down for a while. He is very young," she said. "We started to train the puppies, but they sometimes have accidents."

The puppy barked. He really was cute. There was a bag of dog food in the basket too.

My mom took Mrs. Fox and began to show her the house. After she left, we played with the puppy and made him a little bed in the kitchen. We were up-

stairs getting ready for bed when we
heard a big crash.

"This house is haunted!" cried Gus.
No one wanted to go downstairs.

3

From the top of the open stairway we could see down into the living room. My mom's favorite floor lamp that she got for a wedding present was in a million pieces. It had fallen onto a box holding a mirror. The mirror was broken too.

"I'll find the ghost," I said.

I looked all over downstairs. The puppy was scampering all over.

"I think this puppy is our ghost!" I said.

"Seven years bad luck," cried Marcy. "A broken mirror is seven years bad luck! I'll be nineteen before things get better," she moaned. This was an omen. Her school days in Huckleberry Heights were doomed.

"My lamp!" cried my mother.

"He didn't mean it, Mom. It wasn't his fault," cried Gus. "It's crowded in here."

Pieces of lamp and mirror clung to the dog's coat. Gus hugged him. "Can we call him Smiley, Mom? It's a good name for him."

"He is your dog," said my mother. "You have to name him."

That's how Smiley got his name.

We looked at the mess around us. I shook my head. "I don't think even a little man can fix this," I said.

"Let's leave it till morning." My mother yawned. "We have to get to bed. We really need a good night's sleep."

But in the middle of the night I woke

up. I didn't know where I was. There were noises. One was a click click click. Another was a *hummmm* that went off and on. The drip drip drip I recognized. And then I heard Gus crying and remembered where we were.

"There's a ghost in my room," he sobbed. He was standing at my door now. I could see some shape beside him. I hoped it was the dog. "Can I sleep with you?"

I groaned. He crawled in my bed. It's too small for two people.

I had just got back to sleep when I heard my mom's voice. I thought I was dreaming.

"Anthony," she said, shaking me. "It is too quiet out here. Don't you notice it's too quiet to sleep?"

I turned over and bumped my head on Gus. "It isn't quiet," I said. "There are clicks and drips and hums and Gus and you talking."

"I just hear quiet," said my mother,

sitting on the edge of my crowded bed. I could feel the dog's fur. He was on top of Gus and me. From all the shuffling around he did, he must have figured the bed was too small. He was right.

I felt someone squeeze in on the other side of my mom. It had to be Marcy because I heard that little brush thing she uses to clean her braces go scrunch scrunch scrunch. Mom calls her braces appliances. We call her Tinsel Teeth.

"It's a long way down that hall to my room," Marcy said.

"When we get the rooms decorated, and get curtains up and our little things around like knickknacks and magazines, it will be cozy," said our mother.

I couldn't see how a few china elephants would make it cozy.

"I think we need a decorator," my mother mused, "who could draw things together. We can do that this week."

It was nice chatting here in the middle of the night with the family, but I was sleepy. Just as I gave a big yawn, I heard a loud knock. Then the doorbell rang.

"Now, who in the world would visit us in the middle of the night?" my mother asked.

"I'm not going to the door!" said Marcy. "It could be a stranger."

"Of course it's a stranger," I said. "We hardly know anyone around here."

"I'll go look out the window," said Gus.

Before we knew it, Gus was downstairs.

My mother shouted, "Don't open the door!" but it was too late.

Gus was chattering away to some stranger, and they were coming up the steps.

Now the ceiling light was on, and everyone in Huckleberry Heights seemed to be in my bedroom. Here we were in our pajamas acting like we were having some kind of block party. I pulled the sheet up to my chin.

The man reached his hand out to shake my mom's. "Good evening," he said. "I'm Mr. Otis and I live in the next house down the hill." He pointed. "My wife saw your light on and said, 'I wonder if our new neighbors are having some trouble,' and the neighborly thing to do, she said, was to come and see. So here I am."

"Was a light on?" my mother said, in a high voice not quite her own.

"Mine was," said Marcy. "I turned it on because I couldn't sleep."

"There's no problem," said my mother. "But it was very nice of you to check and see. We are just fine, thank you."

Mr. Otis sat down in the chair near the foot of the bed. I felt like I was in the hospital and all these people were visiting me. I started to pretend my arm and leg were in a cast, and there were bottles dripping liquid stuff into me and rubber tubes all over. "Ohhhhh," I moaned softly. I

raised my leg up, as if it were hanging in traction. No one seemed to notice. The dog licked my face.

"Well, we're right down the street. Call anytime. We're up late, the wife and me," said Mr. Otis. He was a tall man with shaggy hair and wire-rimmed glasses. He looked old-fashioned, like a hippie.

We all smiled. It sounded like he was about to leave, but Mr. Otis didn't move. I thought any minute my mom would start serving him coffee and doughnuts.

"I'm in hardware," he went on.

"Really?" said my mother. "We have something in common! I am in faucets."

I groaned. The two of them talked about fittings and copper pipes and tool-and-die for what seemed like hours. Gus fell asleep. Marcy scraped at her teeth. And I plopped my cast down on the bed. It was hard holding it up in the air with no real wires.

Just when I was going to suggest

we go downstairs where a proper party could be held (why did they have to choose *my* room?), Mr. Otis said, "Well, welcome to the neighborhood. I have a daughter, Daisy, who's twelve. You'll have to come over and meet the family."

Marcy brightened at those words. I supposed now she'd be asking all kinds of questions about Daisy and what grade she was in and stuff. Snore snore. Bore bore. But Marcy was too tired.

Finally my mom went to the door and let Mr. Otis out, and we all went back to bed.

After they'd gone, two things occurred to me. First, that this dog was not completely housebroken. And he was sleeping in my bed. And second, that my mom must have forgotten we had to register for school.

In the morning I found out that I was right about both things. I changed my bed sheets right away. Then I went downstairs to see about school.

"There's no use starting school this late in the year," said my mother. "There are only a few days left. Besides, I need you at home."

"There's a whole month left," said Marcy. "We can't stay home for a month."

"We can help you after school. It's not like we own a farm and you need us to harvest the crops or anything," I added.

Staying home was a tempting thought. It was no fun to walk into a strange classroom. I probably should have let sleeping dogs lie. My mom has a long history of keeping us home from school. If there isn't a holiday, she'll invent one. Like Take Your Child to Lunch day. We're the only kids I know who celebrate Grandparents Day and Groundhog Day by staying home from school.

"We better nip this in the bud," I whispered to Marcy, "or we can forget about college."

"You can strain your mind with too

37

many facts. Reading causes eyestrain," said my mom. She passed me a box of cereal.

Just then the little man came to fix the door and water pipe and leak in Gus's room. My mom went off with him, and I said to Marcy, "We'll have to make some kind of deal. If she lets us go to school, we'll do something she wants."

"What?" said Marcy.

"There'll be something. Just wait."

There was.

At noon Aunt Fluffy came in. "I took a home-decorating course at night school," she said. She wore a bright pink jumpsuit and lime-green sneakers. I liked her style, but I worried about her decorating the house.

She walked around giving the furniture a shove here and there and using words like *private area* and *dreaming space.* She had a little case with swatches of material. We listened to her talk about intensity and light and negative feelings. She shook her head when Mom got out her knickknacks.

"These are personal mementos," said Mom.

"Kitsch," said Aunt Fluffy.

She pushed the couch into the middle of the room. "Do you like this?" she asked us. "It is used to convey an aura of warmth and coziness in a home with an area of free space."

"It looks like it is waiting to be moved," said Marcy.

When Aunt Fluffy told Mom she had to throw out her driftwood from Florida and the sculpture made from old faucets and pipes, I think Mom gave up on her as a decorator. "Let's unpack the linens," she said to Aunt Fluffy, and led her upstairs to convey coziness to the bathroom.

While she was gone I said to Marcy, "You know, the couch would look good right here coming out from the fireplace."

I shoved it into place. "Then we can

put the two chairs across from it with the table in the middle."

"We could get one of those rugs to put between," said Marcy. "Like this." She pointed to one in Mom's *Better Homes* magazine.

When Mom and Aunt Fluffy came downstairs, Mom said, "I like it!"

"It makes a fine grouping for conversation!" admitted Aunt Fluffy.

"And the sculpture can stand right here beside the fireplace," I said, giving it a shove.

"I love it!" said my mom. "You're a genius, Anthony."

"You have natural talent," said Aunt Fluffy.

"I've got a deal for you, Mom," I said. "Marcy and I will decorate the house if you let us go to school."

"I think that is a good deal," said Aunt Fluffy.

"I'll call and register you," said my mother.

When I grow up, I want to negotiate arms control agreements with the Soviet Union. I think I could do a fine job.

4

The next day was Saturday, so we had two whole days before we had to start school. The sun streamed in my window real early and woke me up because we didn't have any curtains yet.

"Hey, Tony! Hey, Gus!" I heard a voice shout. "Come on out!" Then the doorbell rang.

When I got to the door, there was Lenny with his bike. He was all ready to take us on a guided tour of Huckle-berry Heights.

Lenny came in and hung over us while we ate breakfast. Gus went to find our bikes.

When we got outside, Lenny passed out the maps.

"Maps?" I said. "Of Huckleberry Heights?"

"My dad made them at the office," he explained. "It's easy to get lost without a map," he added.

Now Marcy had joined us, with her bike. We all studied the map.

"Is there any buried treasure?" asked Gus.

"It's not that kind of map," said Lenny. "Now, here is where we are." He pointed to the top left side of the paper. "On Tiger Tail Trail at your house, model 459."

He was right, there was our house! Right on Lenny's map!

"Tiger Tail Trail goes all around Huckleberry Heights in a circle, so if you get lost, just look for your street and follow it and you'll be home."

"Johnny Cake Road curves through here, that's where I live. See, here's my house."

"It looks smaller than ours," said Marcy. "I thought it was a 459."

"It is," said Lenny. "My dad had trouble drawing them all exactly alike."

"Let's go, and you can follow the route as I point things out."

"Yuck, this mud is hard to pedal in," said Gus.

Lenny showed us how to ride on the side of the road where it was harder.

"Here's my house!" pointed Lenny as we rode down Johnny Cake Road. "We were the first ones living here, in the whole place."

"I thought the model houses were first," said Marcy.

"Well, after that, I mean. We'll turn

right here on Uncle Sam Street," Lenny shouted to us as our tires slurped slurped along. "On your right you will see the park. At least it will be a park in summer when the flowers get planted."

We looked at the park. It looked like a big empty space.

"And here is the new clubhouse and swimming pool," said Lenny proudly. You'd think he owned it himself.

"It's not open yet, but it will be in summer. Note the glass dome on top so light can come in, even in the winter. Real sun. In the summer it opens up."

"That's cool," said Marcy. "We never had anything like this of our very own in the city."

"Over there on Silver Bell lane is the church." Lenny pointed.

"We'll have fun riding around here when the asphalt is in," I said. "We can really sail over these hills, I bet!"

I tried to picture Huckleberry Heights in a few months, when all the mud was gone. I saw green grass and birds and leaves on the short little trees and babies out in wading pools and flowers in the park. It looked beautiful! We could even roller-skate over these hills when the road was finished! As we rode by them I noticed how bright the houses looked. All different colors. Blue, green, yellow, pink, aqua.

"That's 'heavenly blue,'" called Lenny, pointing. "And that model 88 over there is lime green. But we call it 'slime green.'"

I was glad ours wasn't slime green. My mom said it was called "petunia pink." It was rosy and nice.

"Now we'll see where the school is going in," said Lenny. "I'll give you a head start and see if you can find it by following your map. Go!"

"Is this a test?" Marcy demanded. "I don't like tests."

But she opened up her map and started riding ahead of us. We followed her along Uncle Sam Street to Tiger Tail Trail and turned left. I have to admit Lenny's dad had a good idea. I could see why Lenny was organized. I wished I could ask him more questions, but he was only a second-grader and that made me feel stupid.

When we found the school, Lenny was already waiting by the big empty lot.

"I took a shortcut," he said.

"That's not fair, it isn't on the map!" cried Gus.

"This," said Lenny, "is going to be our school. Right now we have to go to Eagle Point School. It's five miles away. But next year we'll be here."

We jumped off our bikes and let them drop in the dirt.

Marcy and Gus and I were all thinking the same thing.

"What a great place to play Nuclear Holocaust!" I shouted.

We explained the game to Lenny.

"It has to be a place where there is no living thing. Not a weed or flower or snake or anything. You wander around and around looking for food or water like you're the last living person on the face of the earth. But all you see is nothing."

"It's better when it's dark outside," said Marcy.

"It's hard to win!" yelled Gus. "I like to win!"

"How do you win?" asked Lenny.

"Well, you wander and wander, and then finally the one who finds the first sign of life coming back, a plant or animal, wins."

"You have to be sure all the players see the living thing," said Marcy.

"Let's play!" shouted Lenny.

"We have to go home and help Mom unpack," said Marcy.

"We'll play next Saturday," I said.

On the way home Lenny said, "See that house? It's a model 80. A kid in my class lives in one of those. Six families live in them."

I looked at the model 80.

"And there's a 210! There aren't many of those!" he added.

A lady was outside the 210 shaking rugs. She waved to us.

"People are sure friendly in Huckleberry Heights," said Marcy.

When we turned onto Johnny Cake Road, we met a lady walking a little baby in a stroller and a big dog on a leash.

They knew Lenny. "Hello, Leonard," said the lady.

"Hi!" said the baby, who didn't look old enough to talk.

Marcy stopped her bike and bent over and talked baby talk to the baby.

"She's just six months," said the mother, "and she can say hi already."

"Oh, she's so cute!" said Marcy. "I love babies!"

"Do you baby-sit?" asked the lady.

"I love to!" said my sister. Then they talked about how old Marcy was and baby cereal and Pampers, and it ended up with Marcy writing her name and phone number down so the lady could call her.

"Bye-bye!" said Marcy, waving to the baby.

"I might have a job!" said Marcy as we rode along. "I could earn some money!"

When we got home, I hosed off our bikes, and our shoes. We went in and ate more cereal, and I wondered if there were any kids around Huckleberry Heights my own age. Would I always be hanging around with little kids? Lenny was bright, all right, but he was still a baby.

All afternoon we unpacked, and Marcy and I started on our decorating job.

"You do have a flair for it, Anthony," said my mom.

Things did start to look nice. Since you know what the neighborhood looks like, I should tell you about our house. Model 459s have these big fake pillars in front. They are supposed to look like houses in *Gone With the Wind*. You can rent the video if you haven't seen it.

When you come in, you're in the living room, and the fireplace is at one end. That's an optional feature.

Then there's a little dining room, but it has a big round light fixture over the table that shines on our food and makes it look better than it is.

In back of the dining room is the kitchen with lots of shiny white cupboards and a microwave.

Upstairs are the bedrooms.

There's a basement with the furnace

and pipes. It will be good for roller skating, I think.

I notice the house seems bigger when I'm home alone. I walk around as if I'm really in charge. It makes me feel like I've got all this power—like it's just *my* house. Even though other families will move in the other units someday, the whole thing feels like mine.

I wandered into Marcy's room. She was trying to find the right clothes to wear to school. She tied something weird in her hair.

"How does this look?" she asked.

"It looks like a dish towel tied to your hair," I said.

"Dish towels are cool," she said.

She had two earrings in one ear and none in the other. And she had on blue nail polish.

Marcy's skinny and has long brown hair. If she wasn't my sister, I might think she was kind of cool-looking.

Monday was the day after tomorrow.

Marcy and I were probably thinking the same thing. A new school. New kids. New classes. New teachers.

What would it be like?

5

On Monday morning when Marcy and Gus and I stood outside in the wind waiting for the school bus, I saw what my mother had done. She had tried to keep us home from school so that we would *want* to go.

"Why didn't we stay home while we had the chance?" whined Marcy as a bunch of strange kids gathered around us at the bus stop.

"It was reverse psychology," I said.

We looked back at our warm house.

My mom was waving and holding the puppy. Smiley had had a fit when Gus left.

"Hey, Tony! Gus! Marcy!" We heard Lenny calling. He was trying to keep out of the ruts because of his clean shoes. Lenny made me feel less like a stranger.

He put his lunch box on the ground and sat on it. "I'll show you the ropes," he said. "I'll take you to the fourth grade and Marcy to sixth and Gus is in second with me."

"I can find my own room," said Gus. My mom wanted to take us all to school. Only babies brought their mothers to school. I'm glad we talked her out of it.

"I can find my own room too," I said.

"Just because I'm in second doesn't mean we can't be friends," Lenny said to me. Then he hit me on the back. Lenny had connections in Huckleberry Heights.

When the bus came, I followed him and Gus on, and the three of us sat in a seat that was meant for two. Marcy sat in a seat across the aisle.

The bus bumped over ruts and sloshed into puddles. The mud sprayed up at the windows and made the little kids squeal.

We went up one street in Huckleberry Heights, and down another. Up Silver Bell Lane and down Uncle Sam Street. Around Tiger Tail Trail. We rode for ages and were still in Huckleberry Heights!

"I'm getting dizzy," said Gus. He stood up in the aisle. He swayed along between the seats, acting silly. The other kids laughed. Gus could be pretty funny sometimes.

When the bus was finally full, we went under the arch and out into the real world. The freeway seemed so smooth.

Marcy was talking and laughing with the girl who sat with her.

"Tony, this is Daisy Otis. She lives next door to us," she said. "Mr. Otis's daughter."

"Hi," I said.

Now Gus had a friend and Marcy had a friend. I had to be next.

We pulled up in front of an old building. EAGLE POINT SCHOOL was engraved in concrete over the door.

"If you need me, I'll be in fourth grade," I said.

But Gus was laughing with Lenny. He didn't even hear me.

"If you miss Mom," I said, "we'll be out at three. And home in no time. Try not to think about it."

Gus had opened his lunch box now, and he and Lenny were exchanging cupcakes. Then we all got off the bus and stood in front of the school.

"Hey, this kid is in our room," said Lenny, grabbing the shirttail of a boy with red hair and red cheeks. "This is Punkin Head Mahoney."

Punkin Head smiled. His teeth were crooked. He needed appliances like Marcy's. He had a banana in his hand, and a big bag-lunch.

"Punkin Head isn't smart," whispered Lenny, "but he's friendly."

Punkin Head was peeling his banana.

"He flunked kindergarten," Lenny went on. "He's almost nine. But he still reads first-grade books."

"I've got an ant farm," said Punkin Head.

"Good for you," said Lenny, slapping him on the back.

Now Gus and Punkin Head were talking about spaceships and sharing a Rice Krispie bar. I hung around them for just a little while.

"If you feel lonely," I whispered in Gus's ear, "remember it takes time to adjust. In a new place the kids will ignore you, but give it time. Don't start to cry or anything."

Before I finished that sentence, Gus and Punkin Head and Lenny were heading inside, and they disappeared into the crowd of kids.

Well, I was on my own. After a few questions, I found the fourth-grade class and went in.

No one was there but the teacher. She smiled.

"You must be our new boy, Anthony," she said. "The children stay on the playground till the bell rings. But you can come in early and get acquainted."

She showed me my desk and gave me some books.

"My name is Miss Purvus," she said.

She seemed to be normal. Like a babysitter, but a little older and a little more dressed up.

All of a sudden the bell rang and a million kids came dashing in. No one paid much attention to me, they were just clowning around with one another.

"Hi," said the girl across from me. "My name is Lily Camp."

"Mine is Tony Doyle," I said. Oh, brother, a Daisy and a Lily in one day. Huckleberry Heights was turning out to be a regular flower garden.

"You're cute," said Lily.

She was cute herself. I mean in a girl-ish way. She had these bouncy blond curls that looked like springs. Her whole body seemed to bounce. She wore a bright red jumper and white Nikes. But she was a girl.

Miss Purvus was talking, but I didn't hear half of what she said because Lily kept talking to me. When I told her to shush, she started writing me notes.

Dear Tony, one said, *Can you come over to my house after school?* There was a heart sticker on the paper.

"No," I said to her. I might need a friend, but I didn't want a girl friend. It felt like trouble.

"Boys and girls," Miss Purvus was saying, "we have a new pupil today, Anthony Doyle."

Everyone looked at me. "Hi," I said.

At recess Lily hung on to me like a leech. She chattered away nonstop. "I've got baseball cards I'll give you," she offered.

Now this girl was trying to bribe me.

"A whole bunch," she said. "If you come over. I live in Huckleberry Heights."

With my luck she probably lived next door to us. I tried to ignore her.

The boys were all playing kickball, but no one asked me to play. Lily had me trapped. Recess went on forever.

The rest of the day went pretty well. I knew more than they did in math, but they were ahead of me in science. I was just getting to feel like the new school was okay when Miss Purvus threw me a curve.

While we were drawing pictures of explorers, she said, "Boys and girls, I want to remind you again of the father–son potluck dinner on the last day of school, June first. It is important that all the fourth-grade boys be there. It is at six o'clock in the Eagle Point Church. One of you lucky boys will win a new ten-speed bike, and volunteers will sign up to help landscape the new park in Huckleberry Heights."

"Miss Purvus, why can't girls come too?" shouted Lily Camp.

The class groaned.

Miss Purvus started explaining something about a mother–daughter banquet, blah blah blah, but I didn't hear her because all I could think of was, Where do I get a dad for a day? Most of the time I don't need a dad, but at times like this they come in handy.

"Miss Purvus, I don't have a dad," one boy was saying. "Can I bring my big brother instead? He's twenty-one."

"Yes, Charles, if anyone does not have a father, a big brother or an uncle is fine."

The closest I came to a big brother was Gus. And even if he walked in on stilts, he'd look like eight. And Aunt Fluffy wasn't married.

Now I had two Huckleberry Heights problems. I had to find a friend (not a girl). And I had to find a father by the time school was out. I decided to find both of them by myself. I didn't want everyone pointing me out and saying, "See Tony Doyle? He hasn't got a friend, and he hasn't got a father."

I wished there was a place called Rent-a-Dad, like Rent-a-Van or Rent-a-Tux.

I worried on the bus the whole way back to Huckleberry Heights.

6

That night my mom didn't say, "How was the first day of school?" She never asked predictable questions. She just said, "I made a real English dinner. Corned beef and cabbage."

"That's Irish," said Marcy. "Not English."

None of us liked cabbage. It looked kind of faded and limp. But we ate it anyway because Mom had made it.

As we ate, Gus told about all his new

friends. "And I'm the best reader in the whole room!" he said.

"The kids at school dress different than I do," said Marcy. "The girl next to me has this ponytail like the girl on *The Brady Bunch*. They all look so *young*. Everybody wears corduroys and turtlenecks, and here I was in my stonewashed denims."

Marcy looked sad. She picked at her cabbage.

"I mean, I was the best dresser in our other school. No one had a collection of work shirts like mine. The kids here don't even wear makeup. Except Daisy Otis."

My mom made sympathetic noises and shook her head.

"At recess I went into the girls' bathroom," Marcy went on, "and took off my eye makeup and lipstick. By three o'clock I felt like putting my hair in a ponytail. I'm going to be just like *them*."

"I want a hamburger," whined Gus.

"Why don't we have any hamburgers and french fries and malts anymore?"

"We are a long way from Hamburger Haven," said my mother. "But that is a good thing. It gives me a chance to perfect my cooking talents. This is much healthier than take-out food."

Mom's words put us all into mourning. We were trapped now. Victims of our mother's cooking. Good-bye double cheeseburgers and tacos and take-out Chinese. It was a sad prospect.

After we cleaned up the dishes, I followed Marcy to her room. I didn't want to be alone to brood. I sat on the edge of her bed as she picked up her *Vogue* magazine and threw it in her wastebasket.

"The majority rules," she said. "If I look weird and kids stare at me, I'll have to change."

I nodded. I saw that I wasn't the only one with a problem.

Marcy got a big carton out of the closet

that held old clothes. Mom collects them for homeless people. Marcy dug through the box and took out a polyester sweater and a pair of corduroy pants that bagged at the seat when she put them on.

She combed her hair over her ears.

"All I need is a little gold locket with this and I can hold my head up," she said. "I'll get one at the mall tomorrow."

She put on a pair of white tennis shoes from the box and set her black Reeboks in her closet. She stood in front of the mirror and pulled her hair back with two combs. She looked a lot like Lily. But she didn't look much like Marcy.

"It's a reverse make-over," she said.

Smiley walked into the room and growled.

"He doesn't even know me!" said Marcy. "Look at him sniff me!"

"You do look different," I said. "Especially the hair. But it's probably just that the clothes from the box smell different. Smiley's got a good nose."

I went to my room and did my homework. I fell asleep in about two minutes.

In the morning Marcy wore her new outfit to school.

When I got to my class, there was a paper bag on my desk.

"Whose is this?" I asked.

No one claimed it. I opened it up and there was a whole bunch of baseball cards inside. I looked over and saw Lily beaming all over the place and making these flirty little faces. Winking her eyes at me.

"Quit it," I said. Then I thought that wasn't a very friendly thing to say to the only person who was nice to me. "Well, thank you," I said, jamming the bag into my desk. At least I wouldn't have to go to her house to get them.

"We've got a sauna in our basement," she whispered, leaning across the aisle toward me.

"That's nice," I said. "You must live in a model 220."

"Come over and I'll let you use it," she said.

Miss Purvus was tapping a pencil on the back of a math book. That means "stop talking," in any school.

Maybe I should ask to have my seat changed, I thought. Or maybe I could put a muzzle on Lily. I considered it.

Before school was out, Miss Purvus said, "I hope the boys are keeping the father–son potluck in mind!"

The bell rang, and I raced out the door before Lily could catch me.

"Guess what?" said Marcy when we got on the bus. "A couple kids in my room had their hair tied in a dish towel today! And Daisy Otis said she's getting her ears pierced."

I saw Lily get on the bus, and I slipped down in my seat so she couldn't see me.

When we got home, Marcy fished her *Vogue* out of the wastebasket.

"Maybe you can get rid of those baggy pants," I said.

I went and sat down at the kitchen table to make a list of ways to find a father, and the doorbell rang.

"Is Marcy home?" said Daisy Otis.

Marcy ran down the steps, and Daisy said, "Can you take ballet with me? I go every Tuesday afternoon." She came into the living room and stretched her leg out and put it on the top of a chair.

"My mom drives me," Daisy went on. "She'll drive you too."

"I'll ask my mom," said Marcy. "When she gets home."

"Everyone at school thinks you're really cool," said Daisy.

"Really?" Marcy beamed.

Suddenly, Daisy squealed, piercing the sound barrier, and I wondered if she was having an appendicitis attack.

"I cracked my fingernail!" she shrieked. "Look! It's ruined!"

She stuck her hand in front of Marcy's face.

"You can put Emerg-a-Nail on it," said Marcy. "No one can even tell."

Daisy looked at my sister as if she'd cured her of some rare disease.

"I've got some," said Marcy. "Come on up to my room."

What a flake, I thought. But I was glad my sister had a friend.

I went back to my list. I wrote *Places to borrow a father*.

1. Borrow Lenny's father. (But that would be embarrassing.)

2. Go to California and find my real dad and drag him back here for the potluck. (That seemed a long way to go to get a father for just one night. And I really didn't like him very much, so I didn't want to call.)

3. Ask my mom to help me. (But the last thing in the world I needed was to have her get involved and make a big fuss about it.)

The doorbell rang again.

Through the window I saw Lily, standing at the door. I wasn't even safe in my own home!

I decided not to answer the door. I ran upstairs and told Marcy not to either. I went to my room to hide.

Finally the bell stopped ringing, and I could see from the corner of my window that Lily was walking away.

Was I too hard on this girl?

Or was a girl friend better than no friend at all?

7

The first week of school went by fast. On Saturday morning I heard Lenny call for us, and I remembered I'd promised to play Nuclear Holocaust with him and Gus in the school lot.

When we got to the empty lot, we had a surprise.

"Hey, look at that!" yelled Lenny.

"Where's the empty lot?" yelled Gus.

In front of us was a giant sandpit. In

the bottom of it stood a great big yellow Caterpillar. On the sides of the pit were huge piles of sand and dirt.

"They are digging the basement of the new school!" said Lenny.

We stood and looked into the pit.

"Our game is ruined," whined Gus.

"No, it isn't," I said. "This is even better! It's like a big bomb crater. It will be harder to win now. There's nothing down there that's alive."

"How can you win," asked Lenny, "if nothing's alive?"

"That's the idea," I told him. "It's not easy."

They both ran toward the pit, and I followed them. Gus gave a great big whoop and slid to the bottom.

"Wow, was that fun!" he called.

Lenny and I went down too. It was like the giant slide at the amusement park in St. Paul.

Lenny's dog, Gladys, had come with us. She barked and barked when Lenny

slid down into the hole. She was an English sheepdog.

"Come on, girl!" called Lenny.

Gladys looked over the edge and whined a little. Then she jumped in.

"We won't count Gladys as a living thing," I said. "And remember, we have to walk like we're in kind of a daze."

Lenny caught on quick. We all staggered around in that pit looking for life.

"It really is like a bomb crater," Lenny said. "Down here it looks like the whole world is gone."

The sky was gray and cloudy. We couldn't see over the top of the sandpiles. There was sand all around us. It felt scary.

After about half an hour Gus said, "This is getting boring."

"It usually doesn't take us this long to find a flower or weed or something," I admitted. Gus and I sat on a rock, but

Lenny kept walking. Finally he gave up too.

We all lay down on the ground and stared at the sky.

"Just think," said Lenny. "Next fall we will be sitting right here in a desk in the new school."

"In this hole?" asked Gus.

"This hole will be the basement," said Lenny, "where the cafeteria will be."

I closed my eyes and pictured myself pushing a tray with creamed chicken along the rail. Right here. Kids yelling and pots full of mashed potatoes and gravy. Those ladies with white aprons dishing it up. They didn't know it yet, but they'd be here. Right where we were lying now.

I felt like I was a part of history. I thought of the pictures in my history books that showed dirt streets and horses and carts instead of cars. Soon there would be a school right here in this pit, and I would be one of the only ones to remember when it was just a big hole in the ground where we played Nuclear Holocaust. Maybe I'd have a long gray beard and be telling little kids about it. They might even be my own grandchildren! My voice would shake, and I'd say, "I played there when your school was just a hole in the ground."

I tried it out on Gus and Lenny.

"I remember when I was your age," I said in this gravelly old voice. "Back in the old days we used to play Nuclear Holocaust there."

Gus and Lenny laughed. But what if a real nuclear war happened? I decided not to mention it. Gus and Lenny weren't old enough to know how serious life was.

"Hey, do that again!" said Gus. "Talk like that again!"

He and Lenny started staggering around as if they were really old.

All of a sudden Lenny tripped on something, and started sinking. "Help!" he yelled.

I thought he was kidding, but when I went over there, he was down pretty deep. He was sinking into the sand, as if it were quicksand. It wasn't real quicksand, because he stopped. But he was down deep enough that he couldn't get out.

"Grab my hand," I said.

As soon as he did, the loose sand gave way and I almost slid into the hole too.

Gladys stood at the edge of the hole and barked her head off.

"I can't get out of here!" yelled Lenny. The more he climbed, the more sand gave way and the farther back he fell. Gus tried to pull him.

"Don't get any closer or you'll fall in too," said Lenny. Lenny was sensible even when he was in trouble.

"Stay back and we will think about this," he added.

Gladys didn't know what *stay back* meant, and she jumped into the hole with Lenny. She licked his hands and began to bark and bark.

"I think we need help," I said. It looked like this situation was too sticky to get out of by myself, and I was the oldest. I was responsible for these little kids.

"Gus, you go for help."

Gus scampered up the side of the pit onto the sandpiles.

"Hey!" he yelled. "There's a cat up here! I saw it first! The first living thing. I won the game!"

Gus jumped on his bike and sped down the street. The cat was a big tiger cat with stripes and a bent tail. It came walking down the sandpile into the pit.

"Meow," said the cat, rubbing up against my legs.

Gladys hadn't seen the cat. But at the sound of *meow*, she stood as stiff as a board, sniffing.

Lenny grabbed her collar to hold her back, but it was too late. Gladys flew out of the hole after the cat as if she'd been shot from a cannon, with Lenny holding on to her collar.

Before we knew it, they were both out of the hole, Lenny being dragged along behind like a cowboy who'd got his foot caught in the stirrup.

Finally he fell to the ground, and Gladys ran on after the cat.

Lenny was rubbing his arms and legs and moaning.

"I'll get her," I said. "You wait here for Gus!"

"Gladys!" I yelled. "Come back. Leave that cat alone!"

But Gladys only had one thing on her mind, and it was the cat. I went tearing up the sandbank and down the street after her. I had to save that cat or Gladys would attack it.

Suddenly the cat turned into a driveway on Uncle Sam Street, and ran onto a sidewalk and right up the steps of a house. The front door was wide open, and the cat flew in. Gladys charged in right behind the cat.

"Gladys!" I yelled. "Get out of there!"

"Eeeech!" It was the cat. Then there was a big crash.

"I think I'm too late," I said to myself.

If I hadn't been the oldest, I would have got out of there fast. Instead I knocked on the open door.

The boy who came to the door looked familiar. He was in my room at school!

"Hi," I said. "My friend's dog is in your house. I've come to get him."

I didn't know what Gladys had broken, but I was sure I'd find out soon.

The boy had on thick glasses with fat brown rims. He looked like a kid who wins prizes at science fairs. One of those kids teachers love.

"Hey, you're in my room," he said. "You're the new kid."

"Tony Doyle," I said.

"I'm Edgar Allan Potts."

Why did that name sound familiar?

"My dad named me after the poet," he said, reading my mind. "Edgar Allan Poe. My dad's a professor."

We went in the house, and all I could see was books. All over the place.

"My dad reads a poem when he comes home," said Edgar.

Did I hear right? Did that rhyme?

"Gladys!" I called.

"Read a book—I'll have a look."

"I'll follow you, I'll look too," I said.

Oh, no, now I was doing it. Maybe rhyming was contagious, like the flu!

We came to a big sun porch, and there was Gladys stretched out in the sun on an Oriental rug. Right beside her was the cat.

"That's my cat," said Edgar. "His name is Elliot."

A woman in a bathrobe stuck her head around the corner.

"She's as big as a sheep," she said, looking at Gladys. "Is she ours to keep?"

This family was bonkers!

"I've come to get her," I said. "Come on, Gladys." I grabbed her collar. "Did she break anything?"

"She just bumped that urn," said Edgar.

"It's of no concern," said Mrs. Potts. She was petting Gladys now. "She can come anytime. We love canines."

Edgar walked outside with me. I told him where I lived.

"Do you like stuff besides poems?" I asked him.

"Like what?" he said.

I told him about Nuclear Holocaust. He didn't seem too interested.

It didn't look like a promising friendship.

"My sister likes ballet," I said, thinking it might be something he liked because it was sort of a grown-up thing.

"We just saw *Swan Lake!*" said Edgar. "At the Guthrie."

"I saw *The Nutcracker!*" I said, eager to show I wasn't a complete dud.

Edgar walked with me back to the sandpit.

"We could climb around on some of those sewer pipes," I said. "And watch them build the new school."

"That would be cool," said Edgar.

"I'll see you on Monday, then."

Edgar nodded, and headed for home. I took Gladys over to Lenny's house.

The guys were floating sticks in the gutter.

"That cat saved Lenny's life," said Gus.

"It was Gladys who saved me,"

said Lenny, giving the dog a hug.

I started for home thinking about my new friend. Edgar wasn't perfect, but he had possibilities.

8

The next week Edgar and I and Gus and Lenny and Punkin Head crawled in all the sewer pipes, and Edgar didn't rhyme our words as much when he was away from home. Then we played Nuclear Holocaust while we still had a chance. (Lenny told us they'd be putting in the foundation for the school real soon.) Marcy and Daisy played too. When Elliot showed up again, Marcy saw him first and won the game.

Lily wasn't at school for a couple of days, and I could breathe normally.

On Friday when I got to school there was a notebook on my desk. A red one. On the cover it said *To Tony from Lily,* and there was a sticker of a heart with an arrow through it. The heart had *Lily loves Tony* written on it.

It's bad enough to see hearts on Valentine's Day, but on regular days it's even worse.

"Thanks," I muttered through my teeth. I wanted to say, Get lost.

"Miss Purvus, can Tony show me what I missed while I was sick?" she said real loud.

"Yes, Lily." Miss Purvus smiled. I turned bright red.

Lily came over to my desk and squeezed into my seat with me. She was so close, I could smell her toothpaste, and her curls kept springing into my face.

Even after I showed her what to do,

she didn't move. Her stiff blouse kept rubbing my arm.

"Ladies and gentlemen," said Miss Purvus (she thinks it's funny to call us that). "May I have your attention? The school is sponsoring a contest to raise money for the new library in Huckleberry Heights."

Then she told us how wonderful a library was, blah blah blah, and how knowledge was something no one could take away from you.

"And all you have to do to be part of this wonderful program is introduce your friends and neighbors to this opportunity."

She held up a couple of magazines. One had a picture on the cover of a fish with his head still on. But it was a dead fish on a plate, with celery around it.

"Introduce your parents to gourmet cooking, or to this handyman's magazine." She waved another magazine.

"What she means," Edgar whispered to me, "is we have to sell magazines."

"For every subscription you put in someone's home, you get five points," said our teacher. "And when you get thirty points, you get a prize. The more points, the bigger the prize."

Then Miss Purvus opened a folder that flipped out shiny pictures of the prizes we'd win.

I liked the look of the camera they offered. And there was a microscope for sixty points. And an excellent kite.

She passed out order forms and little pencils, and later, in the gym, the principal told us what to say when we went to houses. Polite stuff, like not to yell at them if they say no.

"I want that makeup kit," said Lily. "Would you try to win it for me, Tony?" She smiled at me.

"Oh, brother" was all I could think of to say.

When we got on the bus, Marcy and

Daisy and Gus and Lenny all had order forms too.

When we pulled into Huckleberry Heights, Marcy and Daisy ran toward Johnny Cake Road, and Lily ran down Tiger Tail Trail toward the school sandpit. I made sure I went the other way.

I followed Tiger Tail to Johnny Cake, farther than I ever had before. In the opposite direction from Lily. It was right on the edge of Huckleberry Heights.

I turned in at a house with a brick front and a burglar-alarm system. I rang the doorbell.

When it opened, I said, "A library is very important to a school. You can be part of forming a child's mind by supporting our effort."

The lady stood and listened to me. Then she said, "I'm just here to clean the house."

"Then you might like this magazine called *Women at Work*," I said.

"I don't have time to read," she said, shutting the door.

I didn't realize people would pass up an opportunity like this.

I knocked at the door of another condo in the same building. There were lots of toys in the yard. Bikes and wagons and a swing set.

"Hello," I said when the door opened. "A library is a very important—"

Before I could finish, there was a bloodcurdling scream from inside the house, and the lady said she had to go because her kids were killing each other.

At the next condo I decided to come right to the point. "If you buy a magazine subscription, I'll get a prize."

"Have you got anything about motorcycles?" asked the man.

I held up *Cycle City,* and he said, "I'll take it."

Five points!

"If you subscribe for three years, you

get three dollars off," I said. "And I get five more points."

"Okay," he said.

That's more like it, I thought, walking down the road.

I came to where the street ended. Down a little lane farther off the road was an old white house with peeling paint and lots of bushes and shrubs around it. It didn't look like it belonged in Huckleberry Heights. There was even an old barn behind it. It looked like a one-family dwelling.

I felt a chill go down my back as I went to the door. The mailbox said *Hood*. The house looked spooky.

I knocked. A dog began to snarl and bark.

The door creaked. "Yes?" said an old voice. A lady with white hair opened the door. The dog kept barking, but his tail was wagging.

"Come on in, sonny," she said.

I wished I'd left a trail of breadcrumbs in case I never came out.

"Sit down here while I get some cookies I just baked."

No one else had offered me cookies.

She pointed to a chair that looked like it could be a trick chair. I'd sit down and the floor would open up and *plop*, I'd be in a dungeon where she stored kids till she made soup. I decided to stand.

She tap-tapped away on the wooden floor with her cane and came back with a plate and a glass of milk.

"Hot raisin cookies," she said, handing me the plate.

I got so scared, I backed into a birdcage. A canary started to screech.

"I'm Mrs. Hood and I'm glad to meet you," she said. "Hush," she said to the bird.

"I'm Tony," I said. I didn't touch those cookies.

Mrs. Hood sat down in the trick chair. Nothing happened.

"I love company," she said.

"A library is very important to a school," I began nervously.

"Yes, yes! I go to the bookmobile whenever I can," she said. "Learning is something no one can take away from you."

Wow! She could read my mind.

"Do you live nearby?" she asked me.

I nodded.

"They wanted me to give up my land, when they built the condominiums, but I said no. I've been here for fifty years and I'm not budging."

She was munching a cookie.

"If you buy fifty weeks of *Rural Living*, you get six weeks free."

"I'll take it," she said. "I like that magazine."

She seemed so eager that I said, "We have a special on *Pet Grooming* too."

"I'll tell you what," she said, filling

out the form. "I like to play Scrabble. I will buy one subscription for every friend you can bring to play with me."

Wow! What a deal! I'd have the kite and camera in no time. I counted on my fingers. Marcy, Daisy, Edgar, Gus, Lenny, and myself. "Six!" I said. "And maybe more."

"Wonderful!" She filled out more forms.

"Now, you promise me six Scrabble games in a row, every day?"

"No problem," I said.

I sat down in the chair and ate three raisin cookies and drank the glass of milk. Then I said good-bye and flew out the door.

It looked like I'd have the most points of anyone in the whole school!

9

"I sold seven subscriptions!" I yelled, bursting into our house.

"Daisy and I sold four," said Marcy. "We are going to put our points together and share a prize."

At supper my mom bought one subscription from each of us.

"The Huckleberry Heights mailman is going to have a sore back, carrying all of these magazines," she said.

I told my family about Mrs. Hood.

"Guess what? For every subscription she bought, we get to play a game of Scrabble with her!"

"*Who* gets to play?" asked Marcy.

"All of us."

"Anthony Doyle, I'm not playing Scrabble with any old lady. And neither are my friends," said Marcy.

"You won't help a little old lady?"

"You're a sneak," said Marcy. "I'm not doing it."

I felt nervous. I'd have to take Marcy's turn. And Daisy's too.

"Gus, you'll play, won't you?"

"Sure," said Gus. He squirted mustard on his hot dog. "But then the points are mine."

I was amazed at the insensitivity of my family. It looked like I'd be tied up for three nights.

"Lenny might do it," I said.

"Never," said Gus.

Gus was right, Lenny was a businessman. "What's my cut?" he'd ask.

My last hope was Edgar. I called him on the phone.

"I take violin lessons on Monday," he said.

"You can play on Tuesday."

"On Tuesday I go to Dungeons and Dragons with my dad."

"Weekends," I said.

"I don't like to tie up my weekends," he said.

Boy, I couldn't count on my family or my friends. Was I the only one who took pride in my community?

I almost cried, I felt so noble. A generous heart meant you had to suffer. If I had to play Scrabble every night of the week for the good of the library, I would.

"I'll do it myself," I said to my family with a loud sigh.

Mom said, "Good for you, Anthony. You made your bed, now you have to sit on it."

"Lie in it, Mom," said Marcy.

I went up to my room.

On Monday I missed a skating party after school. I played Scrabble.

On Tuesday I missed a special on TV about killer whales. I played Scrabble. I did learn some new words, and her cookies were good, but Scrabble was getting boring.

Wednesday morning on the bus Lenny said, "I sold twenty subscriptions without going out of my house!"

"What did you do Lenny, telemarketing?" I was getting annoyed.

"I sold them to my relatives!" said Lenny, holding up a fistful of order blanks all filled out. "I've got lots of aunts and uncles."

I'd have to call up Aunt Fluffy.

Gus hadn't sold any. He said he didn't care about knowledge.

Edgar said he wasn't going to sell any either. "My dad doesn't believe in door-to-door selling," he said.

"Free enterprise is a *privilege*," argued

Lenny. "It's the backbone of the American economy."

"And it's for the library," I said.

"My dad says he'll *buy* me a camera," said Edgar, shrugging his shoulders.

I didn't see Lily get on the bus, but before I knew it she was sitting down next to me.

"What a cute shirt," she cooed into my ear. "You should turn the sleeves up, like this."

She started fooling around with my sleeves.

The boys started snickering.

"Tony's got a girl friend," sang Punkin Head.

A second-grader, teasing *me*.

He squeezed in on the other side of me, which made me even closer to Lily.

"She's a pest," whispered Punkin Head. "Do you want to know how to get rid of her?"

"You bet," I said.

He put his mouth next to my ear and whispered, "Tell her you have this really contagious disease, like chicken pox, and she'll die if she gets too close to you."

"It's not polite to have secrets," said Lily.

Punkin Head winked. "Try it," he said.

How did this little kid know so much about girls? His plan seemed a little extreme. But I'd keep it in mind if things got desperate.

"Thanks," I said.

In school, Miss Purvus said, "Attention, gentlemen! I would like to know what kind of food each of you is bringing to the potluck dinner. Could you write it down for me and hand it in today?"

"My dad and I are bringing fried chicken," said Edgar, writing it on a slip of paper. Some of the other kids were bringing Jell-O and potato chips. I better hand one in, too, or Miss Purvus would call me up in front of the room and ask why.

I scribbled *potato salad* on a paper and handed it in with the others.

The dinner was only one week away, and I wasn't any closer to having a dad. I had to face it. I needed help.

After school I consulted Punkin Head and Lenny and Edgar.

"Come with me and my dad," said Edgar.

"I want my own dad," I said.

"There's the janitor at school," said Lenny.

"Everybody would know he's not my dad!" I said.

"How about the bus driver?" said Punkin Head.

I groaned.

"I've got this uncle, but he's in Peru," said Edgar. "Don't you have any uncles, Tony?"

"Not around here," I said.

That night I confided my problem to Marcy, and she said, "I'll be your dad!"

"I need help, not jokes," I said.

"I'll dress up," she said. She started looking through her closet and pushing clothes around. "I can paste on this mustache, and wear a wig and—"

"No way," I said.

"No one could tell," she said.

"*No!*" I yelled.

"Well, all right!" she yelled back. "I think I have a ballet recital June first anyway."

I dashed over to Mrs. Hood's for our Scrabble game. On the way I decided the smart thing to do was to tell her I couldn't play Scrabble forever.

But when I got there, she said, "How about a nice piece of gingerbread? I just took it out of the oven."

"With whipped cream?" I asked.

"And a cherry," she added.

How could I give bad news to a lady

who gave me gingerbread with whipped cream and a cherry?

I didn't. I beat her at a game of Scrabble and had another piece of gingerbread.

"See you tomorrow," I called as I left.

Lily grabbed me on the playground the next morning and took my lunch box.

"Give me that!" I yelled. I started chasing her.

"Come on, Tony, get her!" I heard the kids yell.

I saw what she was doing. She was making me chase *her*. Under the swing set, between the slides and teeter-totters. It looked like I wanted to catch her. All I really wanted was my lunch box.

"She's got my lunch!" I yelled as I sailed by Edgar.

"Sure, sure," he said.

Punkin Head just shook his head at me. "I told you what to do," he yelled.

Lily stopped at the school door and let me catch her. She threw her arms

around my neck and—you won't believe this—she actually *kissed me.* Gross.

The whole playground was laughing at me. I was humiliated. It was time to take Punkin Head's advice.

When we got in the room, I said, "Lily, I want to talk to you."

She stood over my desk smiling. "What?" she said.

I opened my mouth to say, Do you know you are going to die of chicken pox?

But instead, what came out was "Do you like to play Scrabble?"

"I love it," she said. "One time I used all my letters and got fifty extra points."

I told her about Mrs. Hood and my problem.

"I'll play with her!" she said. "That sounds like fun!"

"It does?" I said.

On the way over to Mrs. Hood's that evening, Lily tried to hold my hand. I snatched it away.

"Get real," I told her.

"This is Lily," I said to Mrs. Hood. "She's here to play Scrabble with you tonight."

"How nice," said Mrs. Hood. "Come right in and have a piece of pie. It's a new recipe I tried today."

When I was about to leave, she said, "Tony, will you be free on Saturday? There is someone I want you to meet."

"Who?" I said.

"My grandson. He is coming from Ohio to see me. He doesn't know anyone here, but I think he'd like to meet you."

"How old is he?" I asked, thinking I didn't need another little kid in my life.

"He's older than you are. He's eighteen. He loves to play Scrabble too."

"Okay," I said. I was all the way out the door when I turned around and went back.

"Do you think your grandson would

like to go to a potluck dinner on June first?"

"I'm sure he'd love it!" said Mrs. Hood.

When I got home, Marcy was standing on her toes in her new pink ballet shoes, holding on to the edge of the cupboard.

My mom was pinning up a pink ruffly dress she called a tutu. Marcy was smiling so wide that all of her appliances showed.

"Pretty soon I'll be as good as Daisy," she said.

The rosy light from the setting sun was streaming in the living room windows, making golden circles on the white walls. Gus was brushing Smiley with my hairbrush. I didn't even yell at him.

Maybe I'd win a bike at the dinner. My luck was turning around. I had new friends. My Scrabble term was over. And I had a substitute father.

"Can you make potato salad?" I asked my mom.

"Yes," she said. "I have a good recipe with cucumber in it."

Marcy danced on her toes, dipping and twirling.

Smiley got tired of being brushed, and lay down at my feet for a nap.

"Don't you just love Huckleberry Heights?" mused my mom. "With our whole family nice and cozy together in our new house. I told you we'd love it. It's a real delight."

"Mom," I said, "you were absolutely right!"

SOUP RIDES AGAIN!

Whether he's riding into trouble on horse-back or rolling into trouble on an outrageous set of wheels, Soup and his best friend Rob have a knack for the kind of crazy mix-ups that are guaranteed to make you laugh out loud!

☐ SOUP 48186-4 $2.95

☐ SOUP AND ME 48187-2 $2.95

☐ SOUP FOR PRESIDENT 48188-0 $2.50

☐ SOUP IN THE SADDLE 40032-5 $2.75

☐ SOUP ON FIRE 40193-3 $2.95

☐ SOUP ON ICE 40115-1 $2.75

☐ SOUP ON WHEELS 48190-2 $2.95

☐ SOUP'S DRUM 40003-1 $2.95

☐ SOUP'S GOAT 40130-5 $2.75